To the belief that there are two sides to every story
—F.M.

To Bugsy and Chico
—M.S.

Text copyright © 1999 by Faith McNulty.
Illustrations copyright © 1999 by Mavis Smith.
All rights reserved. Published by Scholastic Inc.
Printed in the United States of America CGB

ISBN 0-439-12401-8
(meets NASTA specifications)

SCHOLASTIC, READ 180, and associated logos and designs are trademarks and/or registered trademarks of Scholastic Inc.

LEXILE is a registered trademark of MetaMetrics, Inc.

9   10   11   23   13 12 11

The Story of a Flea and his Dog

by Faith McNulty
Illustrated by Mavis Smith

SCHOLASTIC INC.
New York   Toronto   London   Auckland   Sydney
Mexico City   New Delhi   Hong Kong   Buenos Aires

Hi there!

I'm a flea named Herman.

Just hold still

while I jump aboard

and tell you the story of my life.

Boy, is it exciting!

One narrow escape after another.

But we fleas are smart—and lucky.

Fleas always win!

I was born in a rug

where my mother laid

a couple of hundred eggs.

I was a tiny little thing,

weak and helpless and hungry.

I ate dust and stuff

and grew quickly.

In a few days I jumped

for the first time.

It was just a little jump,

but I loved it.

I knew I was born to jump.

I jumped again,

so high that I had

a view of the whole world.

I saw an ocean of rug

with flowers on it—

very pretty—

a sofa as big as the Rocky Mountains,

and I saw A DOG!

A lovely, fuzzy, yellow dog,

lying on the rug by the sofa.

9

It was love at first sight.

I hopped and skipped

across the rug.

My brothers and sisters—

I had lots of them—

hopped beside me.

We were almost there,

when I heard a whistle.

A voice called, "Here, Goldie!"

The dog got up

and ran out of the room.

I sat down and cried.

So did my brothers and sisters.

But we fleas are smart

and we never give up.

We talked it over

and came up with an idea—

go to the place where the dog

had been lying and wait!

So we hopped over.

We could tell by the dog hair

when we got to the right spot.

While we waited, we played games—
tag, hopscotch, hide-and-seek.
I practiced high jumps
and quick turns.
But we were getting hungry.
In fact, I was starving.
I thought, *If that dog doesn't come
back soon I'll die!*

Then I heard footsteps and voices.

Goldie trotted into the room—

and then, *(sob!)* jumped onto the sofa.

Out of reach!

We all wailed.

15

Then a lady came into the room.

She said, "Goldie!

Get down this minute!

You should be ashamed!"

Goldie jumped off the sofa

and lay down

just where we were waiting.

Singing and laughing,

we jumped aboard.

Life on Goldie

was wonderful.

She didn't seem to notice us.

We ate well. We played games

in the forest of golden hair.

Then she began to scratch.

It was terrifying.

At any moment sharp toenails

might rake through the hair.

I was afraid I'd be crushed

or flung out into space.

I saw that happen to

a couple of my brothers.

But fleas are smart!

I figured out what to do.

At the first scratch,

I hurried down to her paw.

Nestled between her toes,

I rode along safely

while she scratched.

You've got to admit that's clever!

Then the worst happened!

The boy said, " Here, Goldie!"

He got down on the rug

and was petting her,

when Goldie turned on her back.

We weren't ready for this.

The boy saw a few of us
on her tummy, running for shelter.
He yelled, "Mom! Goldie has fleas!"
"I thought so," said Mom.
"Give her a bath."

The next thing I know,
we're all in the tub.
Water is raining down.
We're getting soaked.
Goldie is shivering
and scrambling.

The boy is holding her collar
and saying, "Be good! Keep still!"
I am terrified.
My whole world is shivering
and shaking and wet!
I see brothers and sisters
swept away — down the drain!

I run up to Goldie's neck,

where the hair is thick,

and hang on.

I'm safe for a moment.

Then soapsuds wash over me

in waves of foam.

I let go. I'm swept down.

I don't know where I am.

There is soap in my eyes and mouth.

"Keep still while I rinse you,"

the boy says.

Clear water washes over me.

I lose my grip.

I'm washed along by a river
that splashes down into the tub.
I can see the hole where
the water gurgles down.
I see brothers and sisters disappear!

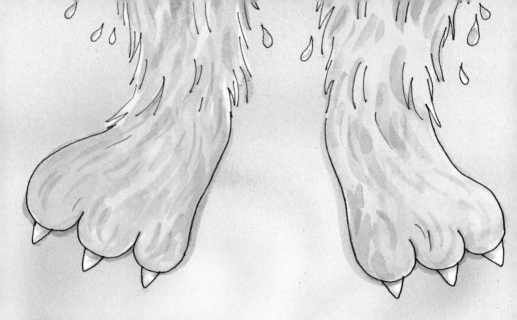

I'm in the water, whirling around.

I think I'm doomed,

but then I see Goldie's paw.

If only I can reach it!

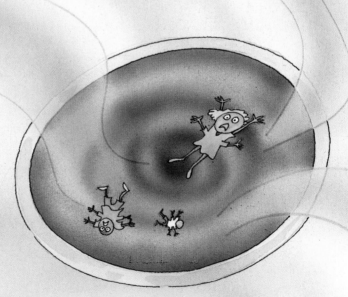

Kicking against the current,
I make it. I seize a tuft of hair,
climb aboard, and hold on tight.

A moment later, Goldie is

out of the tub,

being dried with a towel.

I lie low, hidden between her toes.

When the danger has passed,

I climb her leg.

I run through nice, clean fur

up to her back. I find a few of

my brothers and sisters there.

We all agree it is great to be alive.

The life of a flea is dangerous.

But we are smart. We are lucky.

At least a few of us always win!